ALL AROUND THE WORLD
MADAGASCAR

by Kristine Spanier, MLIS

po go

Ideas for Parents and Teachers

Pogo Books let children practice reading informational text while introducing them to nonfiction features such as headings, labels, sidebars, maps, and diagrams, as well as a table of contents, glossary, and index.

Carefully leveled text with a strong photo match offers early fluent readers the support they need to succeed.

Before Reading

- "Walk" through the book and point out the various nonfiction features. Ask the student what purpose each feature serves.
- Look at the glossary together. Read and discuss the words.

Read the Book

- Have the child read the book independently.
- Invite him or her to list questions that arise from reading.

After Reading

- Discuss the child's questions. Talk about how he or she might find answers to those questions.
- Prompt the child to think more. Ask: What did you know about Madagascar before reading this book? What more would you like to learn?

Pogo Books are published by Jump!
5357 Penn Avenue South
Minneapolis, MN 55419
www.jumplibrary.com

Library of Congress Cataloging-in-Publication Data

Names: Spanier, Kristine, author.
Title: Madagascar / Kristine Spanier.
Description: Minneapolis, MN: Jump!, Inc., 2022.
Series: All around the world
Includes index. | Audience: Ages 7-10
Identifiers: LCCN 2020056026 (print)
LCCN 2020056027 (ebook)
ISBN 9781636900148 (hardcover)
ISBN 9781636900155 (paperback)
ISBN 9781636900162 (ebook)
Subjects: LCSH: Madagascar–Juvenile literature.
Classification: LCC DT469.M26 S866 2022 (print)
LCC DT469.M26 (ebook) | DDC 969.1–dc23
LC record available at https://lccn.loc.gov/2020056026
LC ebook record available at https://lccn.loc.gov/2020056027

Editor: Jenna Gleisner
Designer: Molly Ballanger

Photo Credits: Dudarev Mikhail/Shutterstock, cover; Damian Ryszawy/Shutterstock, 1; Pixfiction/Shutterstock, 3; Gonzalo Buzonni/Shutterstock, 4; Sean Newbery/Shutterstock, 5; ScottYellox/Shutterstock, 6-7; Rosa Jay/Shutterstock, 8l; PetlinDmitry/Shutterstock, 8r; David Havel/Shutterstock, 9; reptiles4all/Shutterstock, 10-11tl; Martin Mecnarowski/Shutterstock, 10-11tr; Eugen Haag/Shutterstock, 10-11bl; Hakoar/Dreamstime, 10-11br; KENTA SUDO/Shutterstock, 12-13; SoopySue/iStock, 14; Dietmar Temps/Alamy, 15; Biosphoto/SuperStock, 16-17; Fanfo/Shutterstock, 18-19; vale_t/iStock, 20-21; Janusz Pienkowski/Shutterstock, 23.

Printed in the United States of America at Corporate Graphics in North Mankato, Minnesota.

TABLE OF CONTENTS

CHAPTER 1
Isolated Island 4

CHAPTER 2
Animals and Plants 8

CHAPTER 3
Life in Madagascar 14

QUICK FACTS & TOOLS
At a Glance 22
Glossary 23
Index 24
To Learn More 24

CHAPTER 1

ISOLATED ISLAND

Welcome to Madagascar! This is the fourth largest island in the world. There are 3,000 miles (4,828 kilometers) of **coastline**. The **climate** is **tropical**.

The island was once **isolated**. It is about 250 miles (400 km) off the coast of Africa. It was not discovered until around 700 CE. People had already been living in Africa for more than 100,000 years!

6 CHAPTER 1

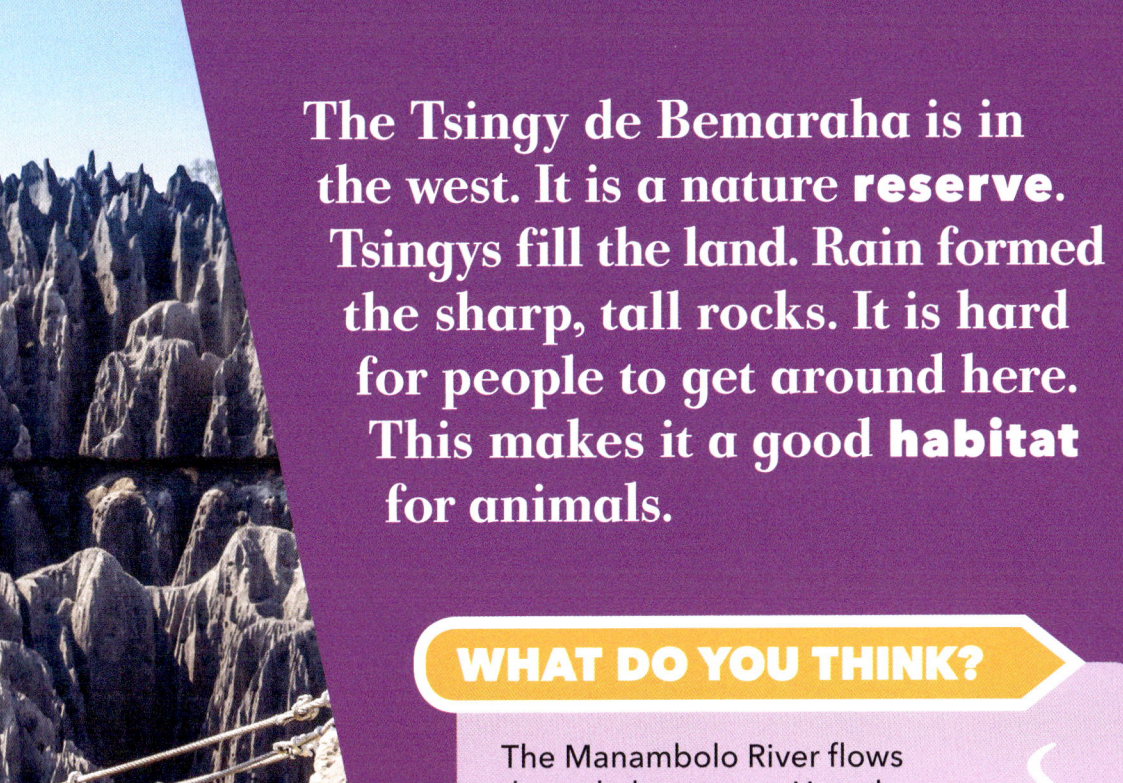

The Tsingy de Bemaraha is in the west. It is a nature **reserve**. Tsingys fill the land. Rain formed the sharp, tall rocks. It is hard for people to get around here. This makes it a good **habitat** for animals.

WHAT DO YOU THINK?

The Manambolo River flows through the reserve. How do you think this helps the animals here? Do you think more areas should be reserves? Why or why not?

CHAPTER 2

ANIMALS AND PLANTS

There are at least 59 **species** of chameleons here that live nowhere else in the wild! This is true for about 90 percent of all animals in Madagascar.

More than 110 species of lemurs live on the island. The ring-tailed lemur is the **national** animal. It has 13 black and white bands on its tail.

The tenrec is unique. Why? It has sharp spines. The coua bird has blue skin around its eyes. The tail on the comet moth can be six inches (15 centimeters) long. The tomato frog lives in rain forests. It puffs up to scare away animals.

WHAT DO YOU THINK?

What animals do you see where you live? What makes them special?

tenrec

coua bird

comet moth

tomato frog

baobab tree

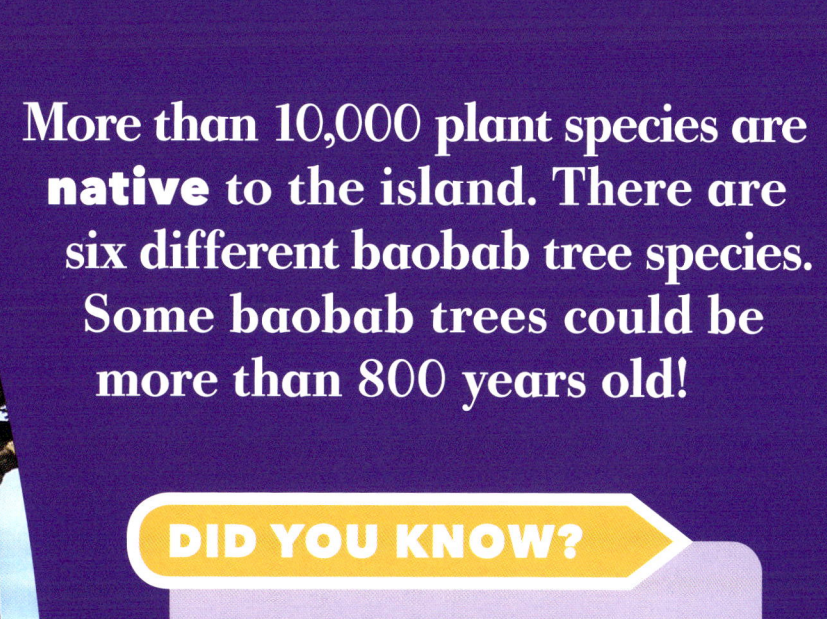

More than 10,000 plant species are **native** to the island. There are six different baobab tree species. Some baobab trees could be more than 800 years old!

DID YOU KNOW?

The baobab tree is known as the tree of life. Why? It stores water in its trunk. This allows it to make fruit during the dry season.

CHAPTER 3

LIFE IN MADAGASCAR

People here vote for a president. The president picks a prime minister. This person leads the government. Antananarivo is the **capital**. It is also the country's biggest city.

Antananarivo

Children start school at age six. Many go until they are at least 13. Some **rural** areas do not have enough teachers or schools. Children help their families farm instead.

vanilla pods

Rice is the largest **crop** farmed here. But Madagascar produces most of the world's vanilla. It comes from dried vanilla orchid pods.

TAKE A LOOK!

Many crops grow here. What are some of them? Take a look!

 apples

 avocados

 bananas

 beans

 cloves

 coffee beans

 corn

 grapefruit

 grapes

 oranges

 papayas

 plums

 potatoes

 rice

 sugarcane

 yams

Many people eat romazava. This dish is meat mixed with onions, tomatoes, and spinach.

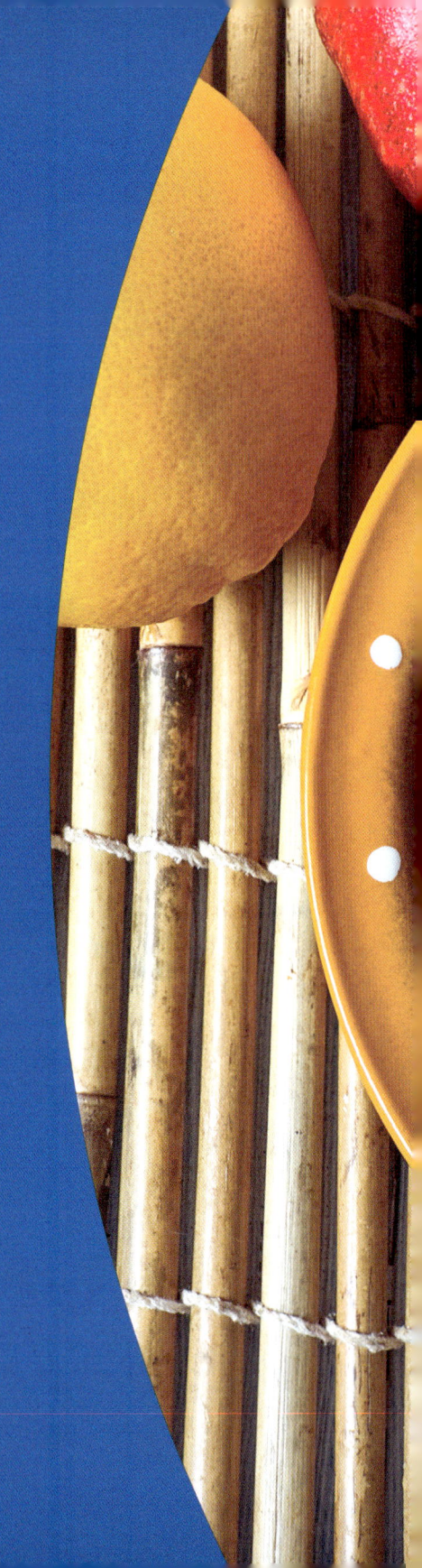

romazava

lamba

Some men and women wear the lamba. They perform **ceremonies** to honor **ancestors**. They make music and dance.

There is much to learn about Madagascar. Would you like to visit?

QUICK FACTS & TOOLS

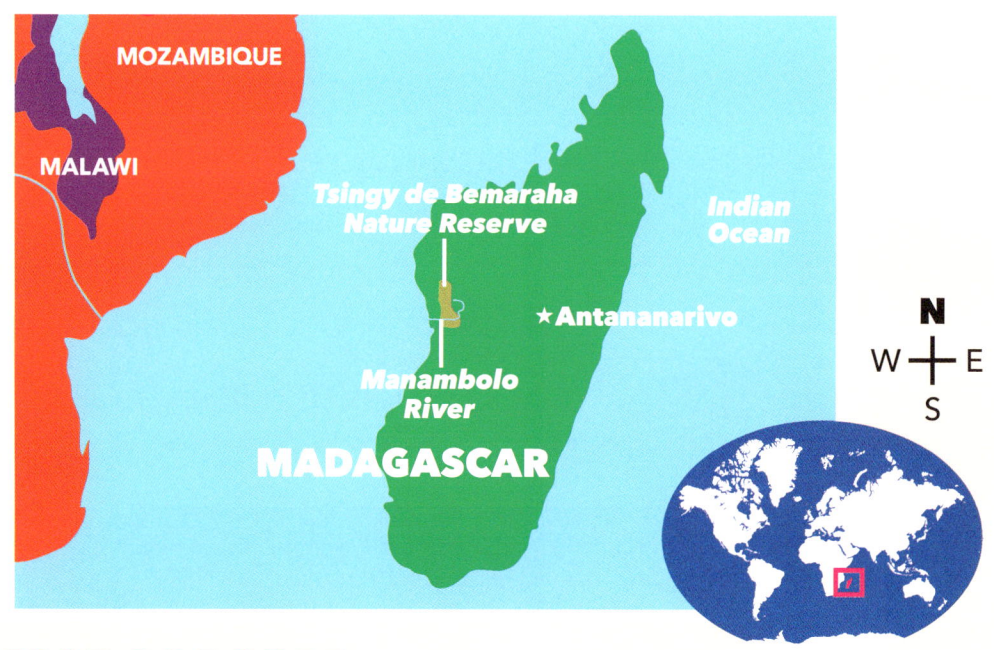

MADAGASCAR

Location: Indian Ocean, off the southeast coast of Africa

Size: 226,658 square miles (587,042 square kilometers)

Population: 26,955,737 (July 2020 estimate)

Capital: Antananarivo

Type of Government: semi-presidential republic

Languages: Malagasy, French, English

Exports: coffee, vanilla, shellfish, sugar, cotton cloth

Currency: Malagasy ariary

GLOSSARY

ancestors: Members of a family who lived long ago.

capital: A city where government leaders meet.

ceremonies: Formal events that mark important occasions.

climate: The weather typical of a certain place over a long period of time.

coastline: The place where the land and the ocean meet.

crop: A plant grown for food.

habitat: The place where an animal or plant is usually found.

isolated: Alone or separated.

national: Of, having to do with, or shared by a whole nation.

native: Grown or produced in a particular region.

reserve: A protected place where hunting is not allowed and where animals can live and breed safely.

rural: Related to the country and country life.

species: One of the groups into which similar animals and plants are divided.

tropical: Of or having to do with the hot, rainy area of the tropics.

Madagascar's currency

INDEX

Africa 5

animals 7, 8, 9, 10

Antananarivo 14

baobab trees 13

chameleons 8

climate 4

coastline 4

crops 16, 17

dance 21

farm 15

island 4, 5, 9, 13

isolated 5

lamba 21

lemurs 9

Manambolo River 7

music 21

national animal 9

plant species 13

president 14

prime minister 14

rain forests 10

romazava 18

school 15

Tsingy de Bemaraha 7

TO LEARN MORE

Finding more information is as easy as 1, 2, 3.

❶ Go to www.factsurfer.com

❷ Enter "Madagascar" into the search box.

❸ Choose your book to see a list of websites.

FACT SURFER